A GIFT FOR

Kaitlen

FROM

Uncle Justin, Aunt Jessica
Jakob and Kelsie

Christmas 2012

THE SOMETHING WONDERFUL

A CHRISTMAS STORY

KAREN HILL

ILLUSTRATED BY
SUSAN REAGAN

CROSSWAY

A publishing ministry of Good News Publishers

The Something Wonderful

Text copyright © 2005 by Karen Hill
Illustrations copyright © 2005 by Susan Reagan

Published by Crossway Books
A publishing ministry of Good News Publishers
1300 Crescent Street
Wheaton, Illinois 60187

Design: The DesignWorks Group, www.thedesignworksgroup.com

First printing, 2005

Printed in Italy

LIBRARY OF CONGRESS CATALOGING-IN-PUBLICATION DATA

Hill, Karen, 1947-
  The Something Wonderful : a Christmas story / Karen Hill.
      p. cm.
  Summary: In a stable in Bethlehem, the animals wait expectantly for
"The Something Wonderful" that they know God has planned for them.
  ISBN 1-58134-732-4 (hc : alk. paper)
  1. Jesus Christ--Nativity--Juvenile fiction. [1. Jesus
Christ--Nativity--Fiction. 2. Animals--Fiction. 3. Christian
life--Fiction.] I. Reagan, Susan, ill. II. Title.
  PZ7.H55283Som 2005
  [E]--dc22
                              2005010507

PBI   16 15 14 13 12 11 10 09 08 07 06 05
15 14 13 12 11 10 9 8 7 6 5 4 3 2 1

For Marco—

You are something wonderful in our lives!

Long, long ago in Bethlehem,
Something Wonderful was about
to happen.

The news spread throughout
the stable.

Dove tuned up her best voice
and sang the news to Rooster.

Rooster puffed out his chest
and crowed, "God is sending us
Something Wonderful!"

Cow told the dusty old camel,
"*Something Wonderful* is coming!"

Camel whispered the news to Donkey.

Donkey told Lamb.

The animals could hardly wait for
The Something Wonderful.

They would crow and moo and bray
and b-a-a-a, all imagining what
The Something Wonderful would be.

Things to do...
1. Parade
   (Camel)
2. Party
   (Cow)
Project Manager (Donkey)

One day, when the animals gathered
to talk about it, something did happen.
But it wasn't wonderful . . . not yet.
Donkey announced plans for *The Something
Wonderful.* "Now, Camel," Donkey said,
"you will be in charge of the parade."

"Parade?" asked Camel.

"Why, certainly. You can't have *Something Wonderful* without a parade." Then Donkey continued, "And you, Cow, will plan the party."

"Party?"

"Yes," insisted Donkey. "You must prepare the food and games."

"B–u–t . . ." began Cow.

"Now, now, no more talk," Donkey said. "Let's get busy. There's a lot of work to do!"

So the animals went to work.

At first everyone got along. Cow helped Dove learn a new song. Rooster helped Camel draw the parade map. Everyone worked hard.

Then something happened.

But it wasn't wonderful . . . not yet.

Donkey complained about Cow's party plans. "You can't serve oats. Some of us don't even like oats!"

Then Camel and Rooster had a fuss about the parade. "You can't have a parade past the water trough.

Someone might stop for a drink and slow up the pace!" argued Rooster.

"And Cow's party table is right in the middle of the parade route!" yelled Camel.

The happy sounds of the stable were gone.
Now the only sounds in the barnyard were sounds of
fussing and arguing. Just then a little voice piped up.
"Excuse me, Mr. Donkey." It was Lamb.
"I don't mean to interrupt, but . . ."

"Yes, yes, what is it? Speak up," said Donkey.

"I was just wondering . . . what is
The Something Wonderful?"

Everyone got quiet. Camel moved closer.
Donkey cleared his throat.

23

Camel spoke first. "The youngster has a good point. How can we make all these plans when we don't even know what *The Something Wonderful* will be?"

"He's right," they all agreed.

"Well, I just thought we should be prepared," Donkey said. "What do you think we should do, Lamb?"

Lamb looked around at all his friends. "It seems to me we should just . . . watch and wait."

Donkey laughed a loud hee-haw. "That's not much of a plan for *The Something Wonderful*."

"And something else . . ." said Lamb slowly. "It seems to me that we should all try harder to get along."

Cow leaned down and nuzzled the little lamb. "This little one is very wise. If we wait quietly, God will show us what *The Something Wonderful* is."

"And if we're more kind to each other, God will be pleased," said Camel.

"Mr. Donkey, I don't think we have to make a fancy celebration," Lamb said. "I think God will give us *The Something Wonderful* just because he loves us."

"He's right," added Rooster. "We can show God we love him by being kind to each other."

So the animals agreed. They would watch and wait and be ready for *The Something Wonderful* to come.

They went about their jobs just as always. But life was different among the animal friends.

Dove complimented Rooster on his early morning song.

Camel shared his hay with Cow. And Lamb
said kind words to everyone. They knew that
someday *The Something Wonderful* would
come to their little stable in their
little town.

And then one night—
one starry, starry night—
something did happen at the
little stable in Bethlehem.
A special baby was born there.
A little baby boy named Jesus.
And this time it *was* wonderful.

THE CHRISTMAS STORY

from Luke 2:1-20

IN THOSE DAYS a decree went out from Caesar Augustus that all the world should be registered.

This was the first registration when Quirinius was governor of Syria. And all went to be registered, each to his own town. And Joseph also went up from Galilee, from the town of Nazareth, to Judea, to the city of David, which is called Bethlehem, because he was of the house and lineage of David, to be registered with Mary, his betrothed, who was with child.

And while they were there, the time came for her to give birth. And she gave birth to her firstborn son and wrapped him in swaddling cloths and laid him in a manger, because there was no place for them in the inn.

And in the same region there were shepherds out in the field, keeping watch over their flock by night. And an angel of the Lord appeared to them, and the glory of the Lord shone around them, and they were filled with fear. And the angel said to them, "Fear not, for behold, I bring you good news of a great joy that will be for all the people. For unto you is born this day in the city of David a Savior, who is Christ the Lord. And this will be a sign for you: you will find a baby wrapped in swaddling cloths and lying in a manger."

And suddenly there was with the angel a multitude of the heavenly host praising God and saying, "Glory to God in the highest, and on earth peace among those with whom he is pleased!"

When the angels went away from them into heaven, the shepherds said to one another, "Let us go over to Bethlehem and see this thing that has happened, which the Lord has made known to us." And they went with haste and found Mary and Joseph, and the baby lying in a manger.

And when they saw it, they made known the saying that had been told them concerning this child. And all who heard it wondered at what the shepherds told them.

But Mary treasured up all these things, pondering them in her heart. And the shepherds returned, glorifying and praising God for all they had heard and seen, as it had been told them.